HORRiD HENRY
and
MOODY MARGARET

HORRiD HENRY
and
MOODY
MARGARET

Francesca Simon
Illustrated by Tony Ross

Orion
Children's Books

Horrid Henry and Moody Margaret originally appeared in
Horrid Henry first published in Great Britain in 1994 by Orion
Children's Books
This edition first published in Great Britain in 2010
by Orion Children's Books
a division of the Orion Publishing Group Ltd
Orion House
5 Upper Saint Martin's Lane
London WC2H 9EA
An Hachette UK Company

1 3 5 7 9 10 8 6 4 2

Text © Francesca Simon 1994
Illustrations © Tony Ross 2010

The right of Francesca Simon and Tony Ross to be identified
as author and illustrator of this work has been asserted.

The Orion Publishing Group's policy is to use papers that
are natural, renewable and recyclable products and made
from wood grown in sustainable forests. The logging and
manufacturing processes are expected to conform to the
environmental regulations of the country of origin.

A catalogue record for this book is available from the British Library.

ISBN 978 1 4440 0112 9

Printed and bound in China

www.orionbooks.co.uk
www.horridhenry.co.uk

*For Robert Ellsberg and Andy Gilbert –
the first Glop-makers*

Look out for . . .

Don't Be Horrid, Henry!
Horrid Henry's Birthday Party
Horrid Henry's Holiday
Horrid Henry's Underpants
Horrid Henry Gets Rich Quick
Horrid Henry and the Football Fiend
Horrid Henry's Nits

There are many more
Horrid Henry books available.

For a complete list visit
www.horridhenry.co.uk
or
www.orionbooks.co.uk.

Contents

Chapter 1   11

Chapter 2   17

Chapter 3   23

Chapter 4   31

Chapter 5   39

Chapter 6   49

Chapter 1

"I'm Captain Hook!"

"No, I'm Captain Hook!"

"I'm Captain Hook,"
said Horrid Henry.

"I'm Captain Hook,"
said Moody Margaret.

They glared at each other.
"It's *my* hook,"
said Moody Margaret.

Moody Margaret lived next door.
She did not like Horrid Henry,
and Horrid Henry did not like her.

But when Rude Ralph was busy,

Clever Clare had flu,

and Sour Susan was her enemy,

Margaret would jump over the wall
to play with Henry.

"Actually, it's my turn to be Hook now," said Perfect Peter. "I've been the prisoner for such a long time."

"Prisoner, be quiet!" said Henry.

"Prisoner, walk the plank!" said Margaret.

"But I've walked it fourteen times already," said Peter. "Please can I be Hook now?"

"No, by thunder!" said Moody Margaret. "Now out of my way, worm!" And she swashbuckled across the deck, waving her hook and clutching her sword and dagger.

Chapter 2

Margaret had eyepatches and skulls and crossbones and plumed hats and cutlasses and sabres and snickersnees.

Henry had a stick.
This was why Henry played
with Margaret.

But Henry had to do terrible things before playing with Margaret's swords. Sometimes he had to sit and wait while she read a book. Sometimes he had to play 'Mums and Dads' with her.

Worst of all (please don't tell anyone), sometimes he had to be the baby.

Henry never knew what Margaret would do. When he put a spider on her arm, Margaret laughed.

When he pulled her hair, Margaret pulled his harder.

When Henry screamed, Margaret would scream louder.

Or she would sing.
Or pretend not to hear.

Sometimes Margaret was fun.
But most of the time she was
a moody old grouch.

Chapter 3

"I won't play if I can't be Hook,"
said Horrid Henry.

Margaret thought for a moment.

"We can both be Captain Hook,"
she said.

"But we only have one hook,"
said Henry.

"Which I haven't played with yet,"
said Peter.

"BE QUIET, prisoner!"
shouted Margaret.

"Mr Smee, take him to jail."

"No," said Henry.

"You will get your reward,
Mr Smee," said the Captain,
waving her hook.

Mr Smee dragged the prisoner
to the jail.

"If you're very quiet, prisoner, then you will be freed and you can be a pirate too," said Captain Hook.

"Now give me the hook," said Mr Smee.

The Captain reluctantly handed it over.

"Now I'm Captain Hook and you're Mr Smee," shouted Henry. "I order everyone to walk the plank!"

"I'm sick of playing pirates," said Margaret. "Let's play something else."

Henry was furious. That was just like Moody Margaret.

"Well, I'm playing pirates," said Henry.

"Well I'm not," said Margaret.
"Give me back my hook."

"No," said Henry.

Moody Margaret opened her mouth
and screamed.

Once Margaret started screaming
she could go on and on and on.
Henry gave her the hook.
Margaret smiled.

Chapter 4

"I'm hungry," Margaret said.
"Got anything to eat?"

Henry had

three
bags of crisps

and
seven
chocolate biscuits
hidden in his room,

but he certainly wasn't going
to share them with Margaret.

"You can have a radish," said Henry.

"What else?" said Margaret.

"A carrot," said Henry.

"What else?" said Margaret.

"Something special that only
I can make," said Henry.

"What's in it?" asked Margaret.

"That's a secret," said Henry.

"I bet it's yucky," said Margaret.
"Of course it's yucky," said Henry.

"I can make
the yuckiest Glop of all,"
said Margaret.

"That's because you don't know
anything. No one can make
yuckier Glop than I can."

"I **dare** you to eat Glop,"
said Margaret.

"I **double dare**
you back," said Henry.
"Dares go first."

Margaret stood up very straight.
"All right," said Margaret.
"Glop starts with snails and worms."

And she started poking
under the bushes.
"Got one!" she shouted,
holding up a fat snail.

"Now for some worms,"
said Margaret.
She got down on her hands and
knees and started digging a hole.

"You can't put anything from
outside into Glop," said Henry
quickly. "Only stuff in the kitchen."

Margaret looked at Henry.
"I thought we were making
Glop," she said.

"We are," said Henry. "My way,
because it's *my* house."

Chapter 5

Horrid Henry and Moody Margaret
went into the gleaming white kitchen.
Henry got out two wooden mixing
spoons and a giant red bowl.

"I'll start," said Henry.
He went to the cupboard and
opened the doors wide.

"Porridge!" said Henry.
And he poured some into the bowl.

Margaret opened the fridge
and looked inside. She grabbed
a small container.
"Soggy semolina!" shouted Margaret.
Into the bowl it went.

"And ketchup!" shouted Henry.

He squirted in the ketchup until
the bottle was empty.

"Now, mix!" said Margaret.

Horrid Henry and Moody Margaret
grabbed hold of their spoons with
both hands. Then they plunged the
spoons into the Glop and began
to stir.

It was hard heavy work.
Faster and faster, harder and harder
they stirred.

There was Glop on the ceiling.

There was Glop on the floor.

There was Glop
on the clock,

and Glop
on the door.

Margaret's hair was covered in Glop.

So was Henry's face.

Margaret looked into the bowl.
She had never seen anything
so yucky in her life.

"It's ready," she said.

Chapter 6

Horrid Henry and Moody Margaret
carried the Glop to the table.

Then they sat down and stared at the

sloppy, slimy,
sludgy,
sticky,
smelly, gooey,
gluey, gummy,
greasy,
gloopy
Glop.

"Right," said Henry.
"Who's going to eat some first?"

There was a very long pause.
Henry looked at Margaret.
Margaret looked at Henry.

"Me," said Margaret.
"I'm not scared."

She scooped up a large spoonful
and stuffed it in her mouth.
Then she swallowed. Her face went
pink and purple and green.

"How does it taste?" said Henry.

"Good," said Margaret,
trying not to choke.

"Have some more then," said Henry.

"Your turn first," said Margaret.

Henry sat for a moment and looked
at the Glop.

"My mum doesn't like me to eat
between meals," said Henry.

"HENRY!"
hissed Moody Margaret.

Henry took a tiny spoonful.

"More!"
said Margaret.

Henry took a tiny bit more.

The Glop wobbled
lumpily on his spoon.

It looked like ...

Henry did not want to think about
what it looked like.
He closed his eyes and brought the
spoon to his mouth.

"Ummm, yummm,"
said Henry.

"You didn't eat any," said Margaret.
"That's not fair."

She scooped up some Glop
and . . .

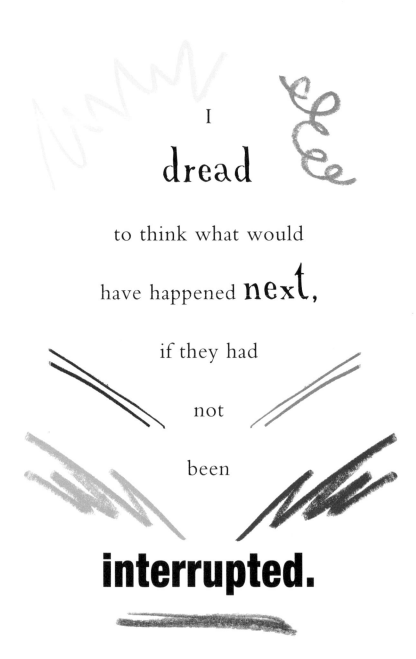

I

dread

to think what would

have happened next,

if they had

not

been

interrupted.

"Can I come in now?"
called a small voice from outside.
"It's my turn to be Hook."

Horrid Henry had forgotten
all about Perfect Peter.
"OK," shouted Henry.

Peter came to the door.
"I'm hungry," he said.

"Come in, Peter," said Henry
sweetly. "Your dinner is
on the table."